CHOO CHOO

SIZZLE SIZZLE

KNOCK
KNOCK

POP POP

BUZZ
BUZZ

MOO

KLOPP KLOPP

SLURP
SLURP
SLURP

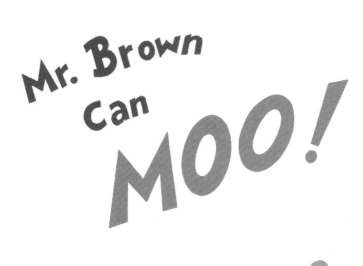

Mr. Brown Can MOO! Can You?

By Dr. Seuss

A Bright & Early Book

RANDOM HOUSE / NEW YORK

www.randomhouse.com/seussville

This title was originally catalogued by the Library of Congress as follows:
Seuss, Dr.   Mr. Brown can moo! Can you?   New York, Random House
[c1970]   [27p.]   col. illus.   24 cm.   (A Bright and early book)
Mr. Brown is expert at imitating all sorts of noises.
1. Sounds—Fiction   2. Stories in rhyme.
I. Title.   PZ8.3.G276Mi   [E]   73-117538
ISBN 0-394-80622-0 (trade) ; 0-394-90622-5 (lib. bdg.)

Printed in the United States of America

MOO

Oh, the wonderful things
Mr. Brown can do!
He can go like a cow.
He can go **MOO MOO**
Mr. Brown can do it.
How about you?

He can go like a bee.

Mr. Brown can

BUZZ

How about you?
Can you go

BUZZ
BUZZ

He can go
like a cork . . . .

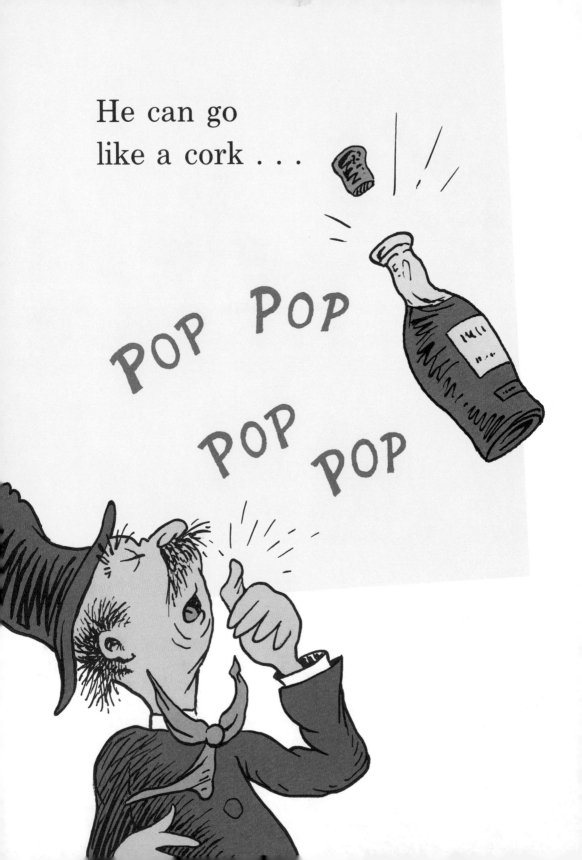

He can go like horse feet

KLOPP
KLOPP
KLOPP

He can go

**EEK
EEK**

like a squeaky shoe.

He can go
like a rooster . . .

COCK A
DOODLE
DOO

He can go
like an owl . . .

HOO HOO

HOO HOO

EEK EEK
EEK EEK
COCK-A-DOODLE-DOO
HOO HOO HOO HOO

How about you?

He can go
like the rain . . . .

DIBBLE DIBBLE
DIBBLE DOPP

He can go like a train

CHOO CHOO
CHOO
CHOO

Oh, the wonderful things
Mr. Brown can do!

MOO MOO
BUZZ BUZZ
POP POP POP
EEK EEK
HOO HOO
KLOPP KLOPP KLOPP
DIBBLE DIBBLE
DOPP DOPP
COCK-A-DOODLE-DOO

Mr. Brown can do it.
How about you?

Mr. Brown
can

WHISPER WHISPER

. . . very soft
very high . . .

. . . like the soft,
soft whisper
of a butterfly.

Maybe YOU can, too.
I think you ought to try.

He can go
like a horn. . .

BLURP
BLURP
BLURP
BLURP

. . . like a big cat drinking

SLURP
SLURP
SLURP

He can go like a clock.
He can

TICK

He can

TOCK

He can go
like a hand
on a door . . .

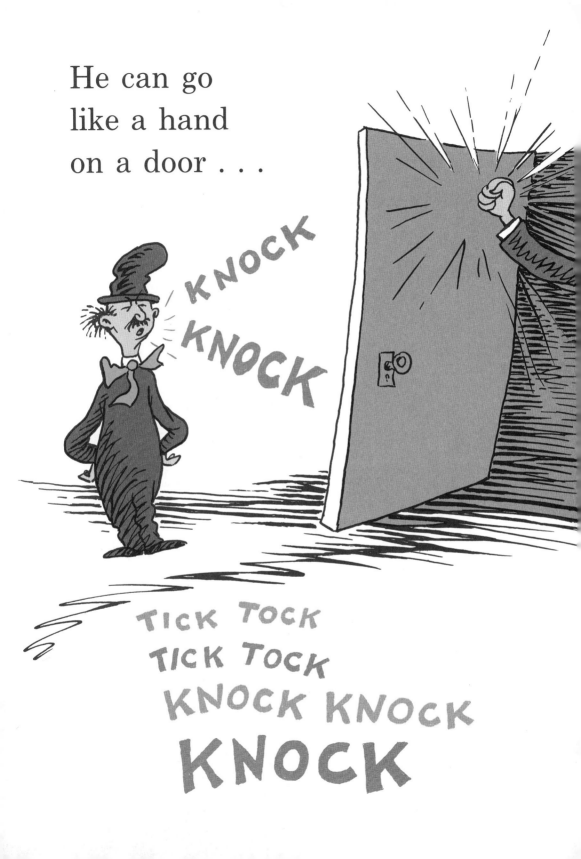

Oh, the wonderful things
Mr. Brown can do!

BLURP BLURP
SLURP SLURP

COCK-A-DOODLE-DOO

KNOCK KNOCK KNOCK

and HOO HOO HOO

He can even

SIZZLE
SIZZLE

He can do that, too,
like an egg
in a frying pan.
How about you?

Mr. Brown is smart,
as smart as they come!
He can do
a hippopotamus
chewing gum!

Mr. Brown is
so smart
he can even do this:
he can even
make a noise
like a goldfish kiss!

BOOM BOOM BOOM

Mr. Brown is a wonder!

BOOM BOOM BOOM

Mr. Brown makes thunder!

He makes lightning!

SPLATT SPLATT SPLATT

And it's very, very hard
to make a noise like that.

Oh, the wonderful things
Mr. Brown can do!

Moo Moo
Buzz Buzz
Pop Pop Pop

   Eek Eek
   Hoo Hoo
   Klopp Klopp Klopp

Dibble Dibble
Dopp Dopp
Cock-a-Doodle-Doo

   Grum Grum
   Grum Grum
   Choo Choo Choo

Boom Boom
Splatt Splatt
Tick Tick Tock

   Sizzle Sizzle
   Blurp Blurp
   Knock Knock Knock

A Slurp and a Whisper
and a Fish Kiss, too.

Mr. Brown can do it.
How about YOU?

EEK EEK

COCK A DOODLE DOO

BOOM BOOM BOOM

BLURP BLURP

9/14/18

DBLE BLE

DOPP

UM UM

SPLATT

Do HOO